MW01434834

A TEMPLAR BOOK

Devised and produced by The Templar Company plc, Pippbrook
Mill, London Road, Dorking, Surrey RH4 1JE, Great Britain.

First published in the USA by Bell Books, Boyds Mills Press Inc.,
A Highlights Company, 910 Church Street, Honesdale, PA 18431.

This edition © 1991 by The Templar Company plc

All rights reserved. No part of this publication may be reproduced,
stored in a retrieval system, or transmitted in any form or
by any means, electronic, mechanical, photocopying,
recording or otherwise, without the prior permission of
the publishers and the copyright holders.

Designed by Philip Hargraves
Color separations by Positive Colour, Maldon, Essex
Printed and bound by Tien Wah Press, Singapore

Publisher Cataloging-in-Publication Data

Wood, A.J.
Amazing animals/A.J. Wood; Illustrated by Helen Ward.
24 p.: ill.; cm.
Summary: Ten animals are boldly illustrated, each accompanied by
a simple, poetic narrative of their behavior.
ISBN: 1-878093-46-0
1. Animals-Juvenile Literature. [1. Animals.] I. Helen Ward. II. Title.
591-dc20   1991
Library of Congress Catalog Card Number: 90-085906

Helen Ward's
Amazing Animals

with text by A.J. Wood

BELL
BOOKS

Here is the tiger,
fierce and beautiful,
stalking his prey
deep in the forest.

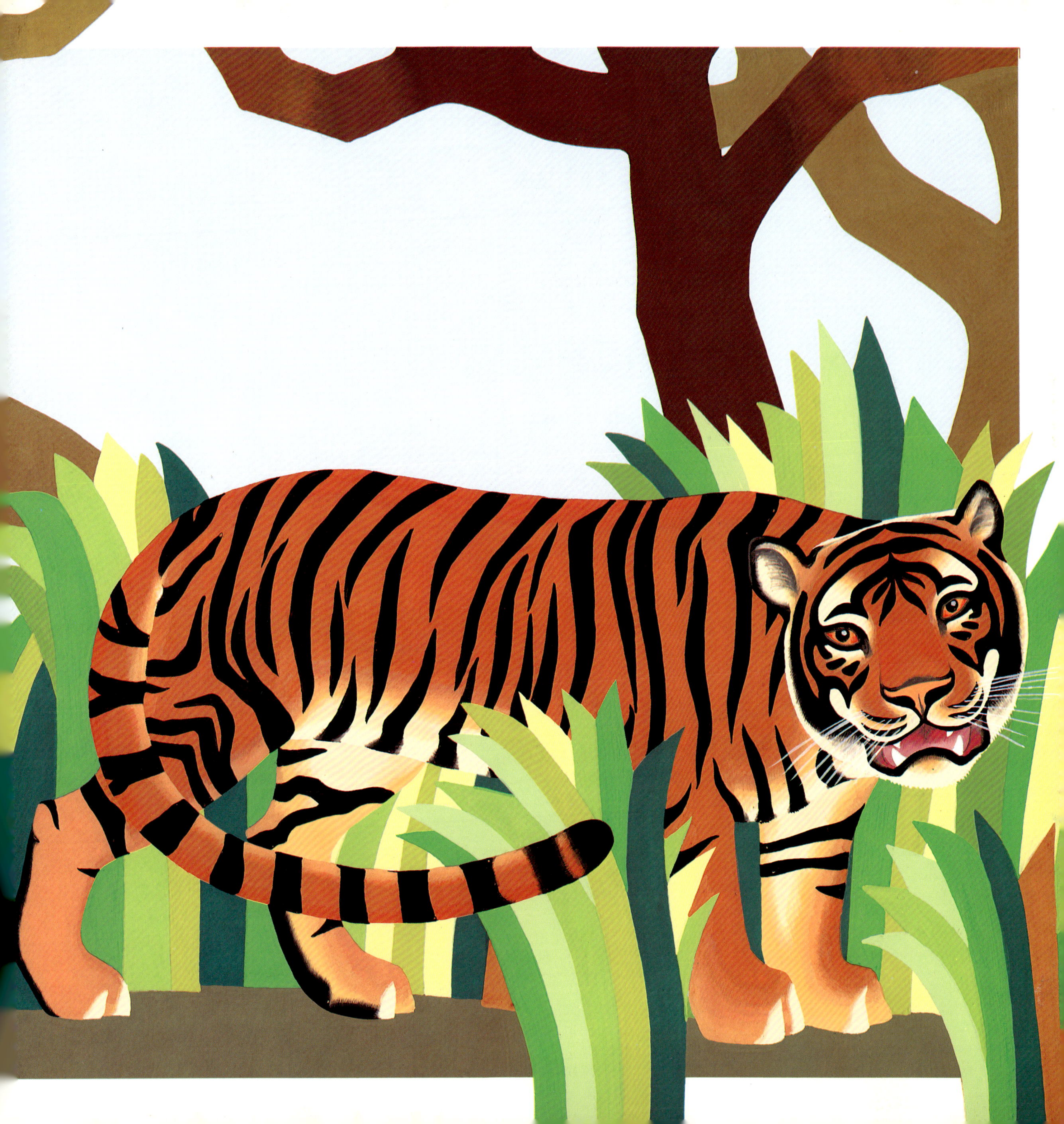

Here are the elephants,
giants of Africa,
lumbering slowly
across the plains.

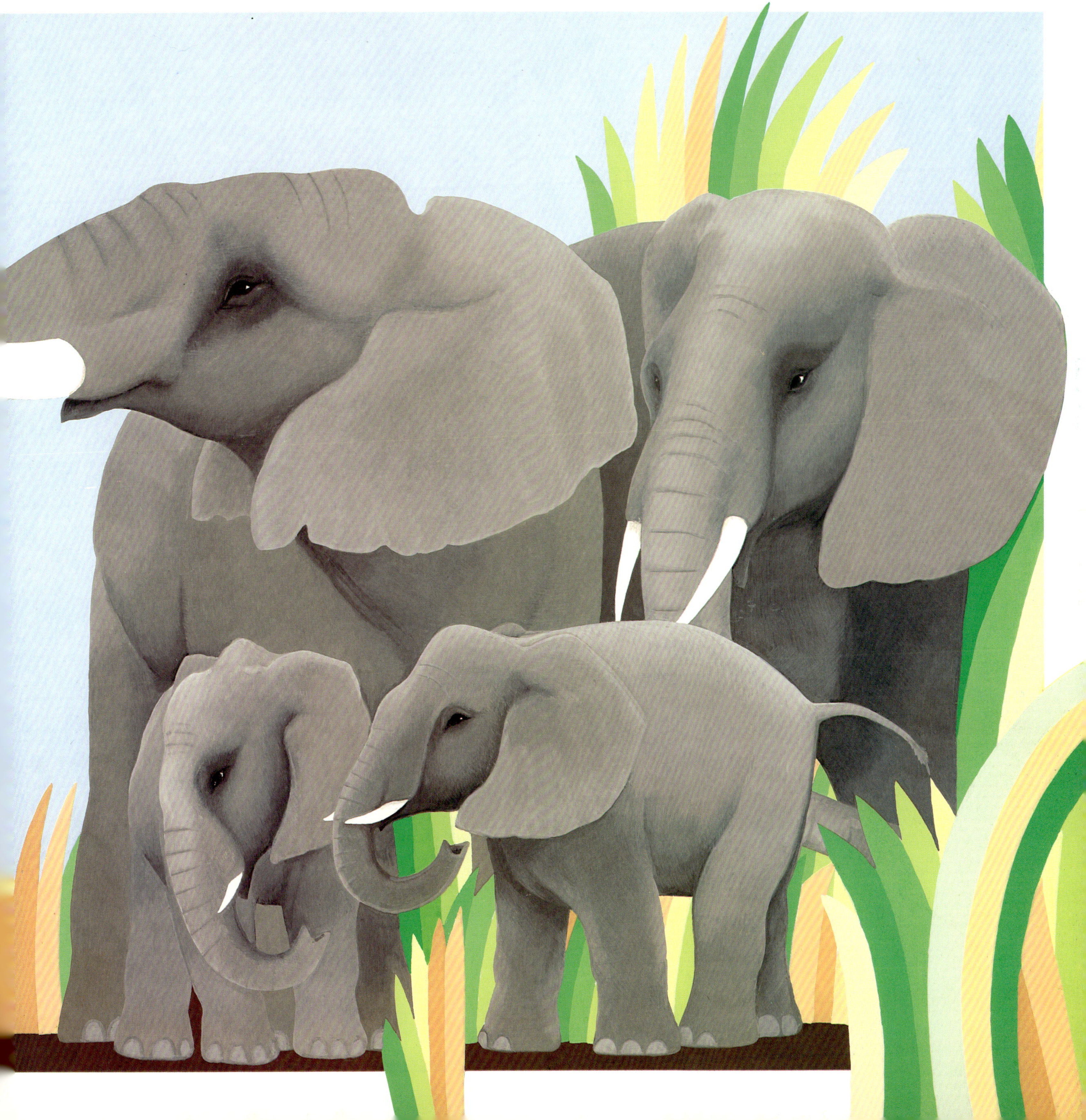

Here are four monkeys, chattering loudly, chasing each other around and around.

Here are two bear cubs, brother and sister, playing together among the trees.

Here is the jaguar,
black as the darkness,
padding softly between
the flowers.

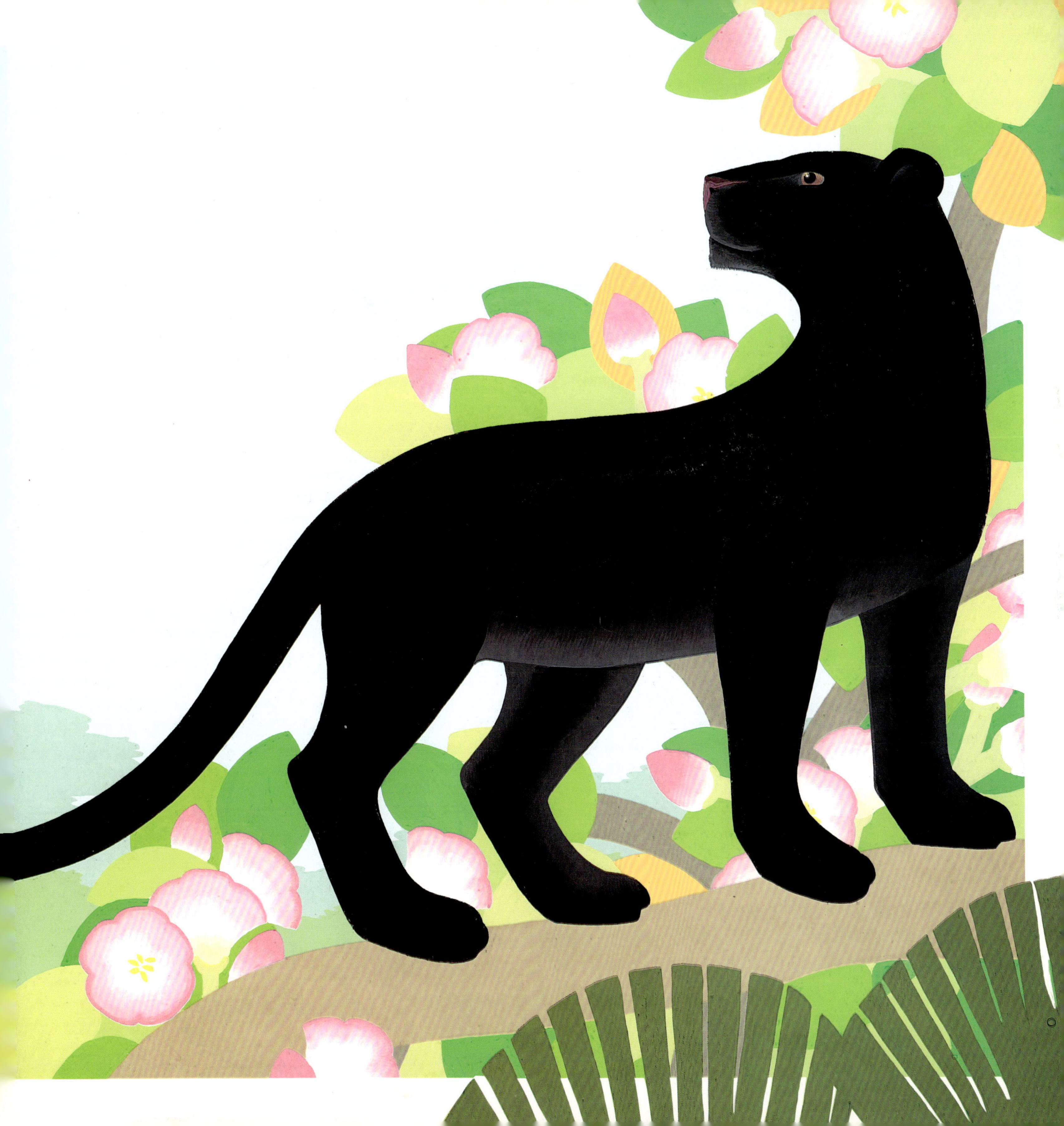

Here is the panda,
munching and crunching,
eating his lunch of
a stick of bamboo.

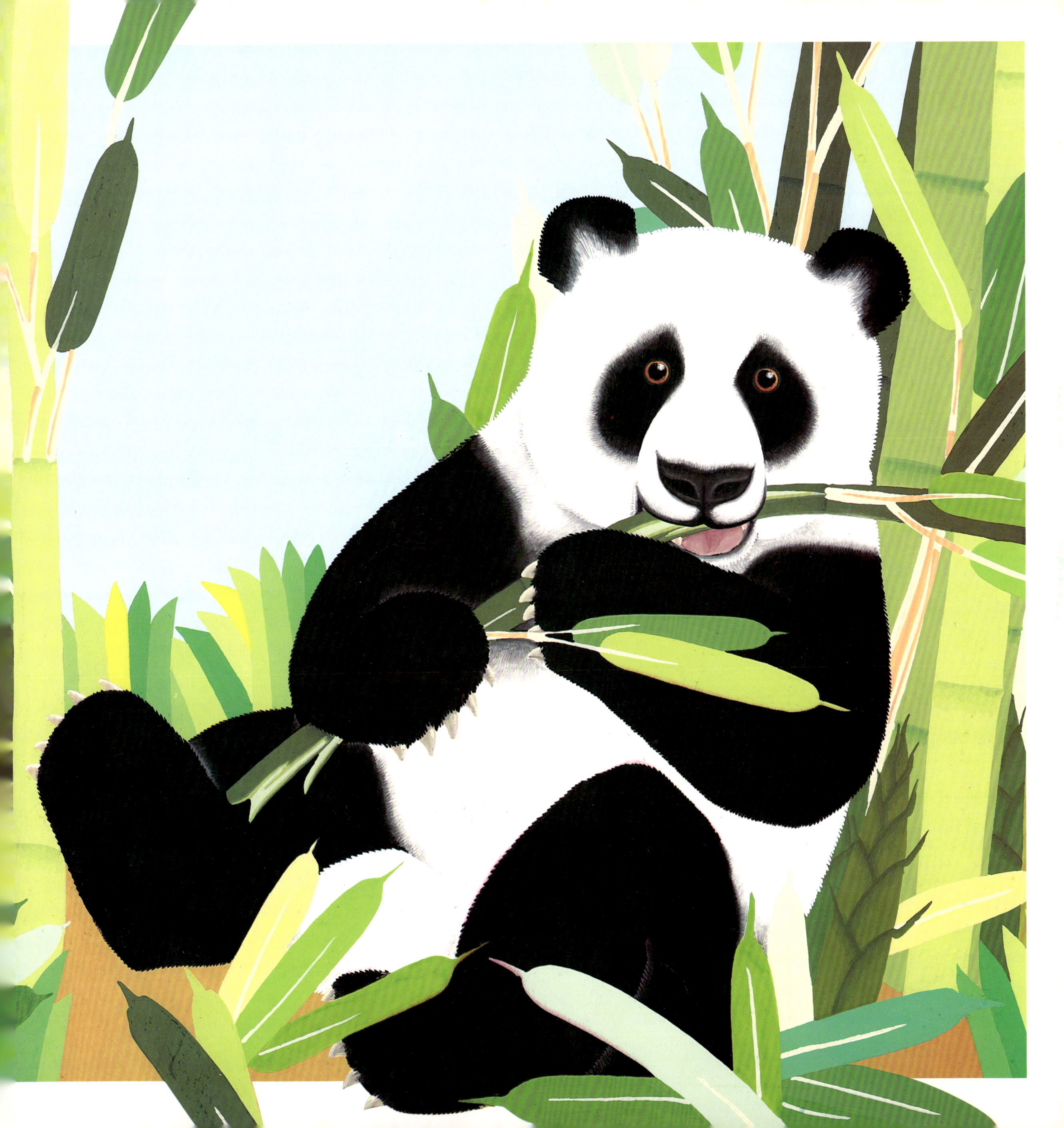

Here come the giraffes,
tall as the treetops,
mother and father
and baby behind.

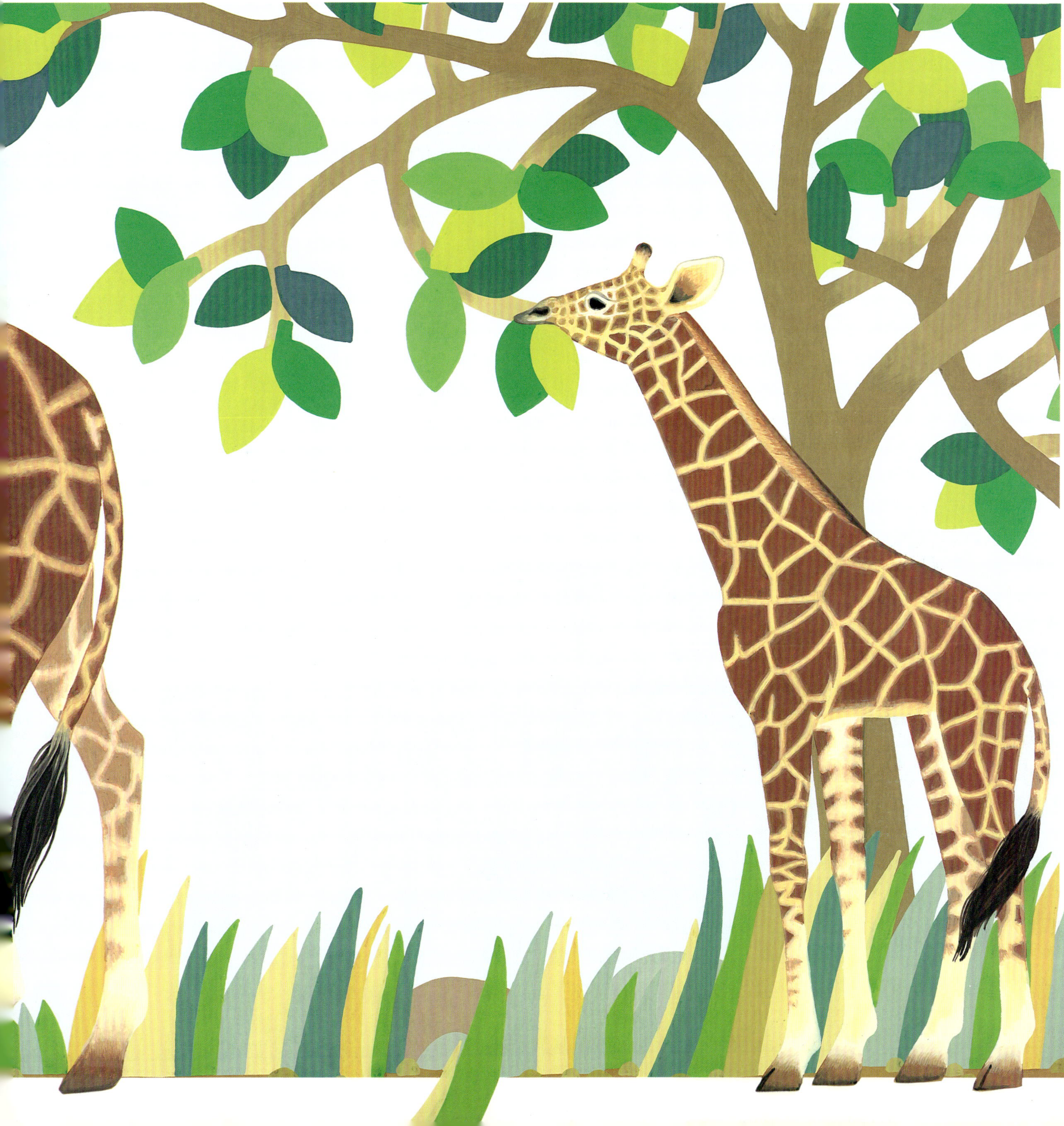

Here are the fruit bats, hanging upside down, waiting for night-time when they will fly.

Here is the wolf, watchful and waiting, looking to see who is passing his lair.

And who will you find down by the riverbank?
Two happy animals if you just look.
Slipping and sliding into the water,
go two playful otters to finish this book.

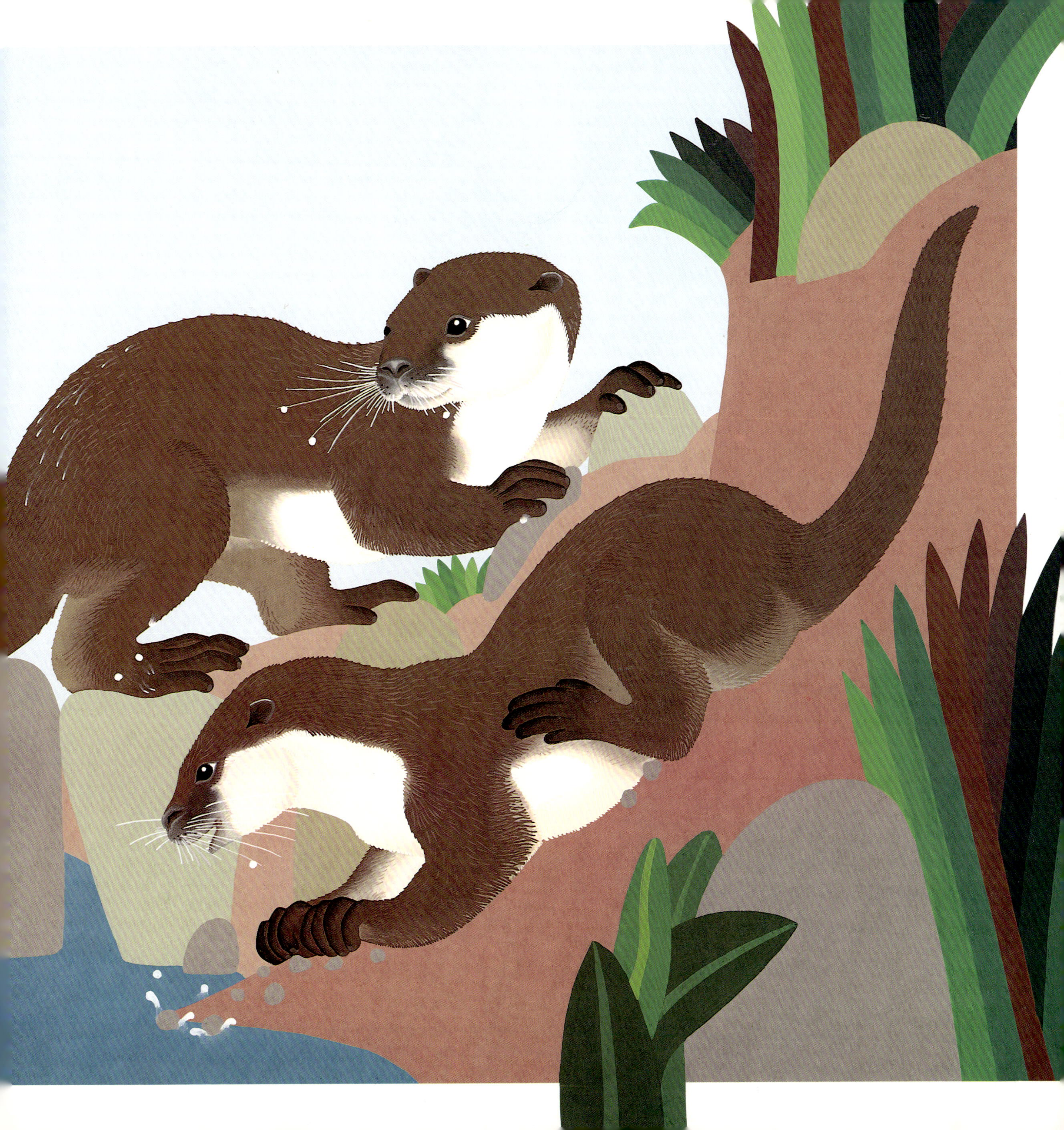

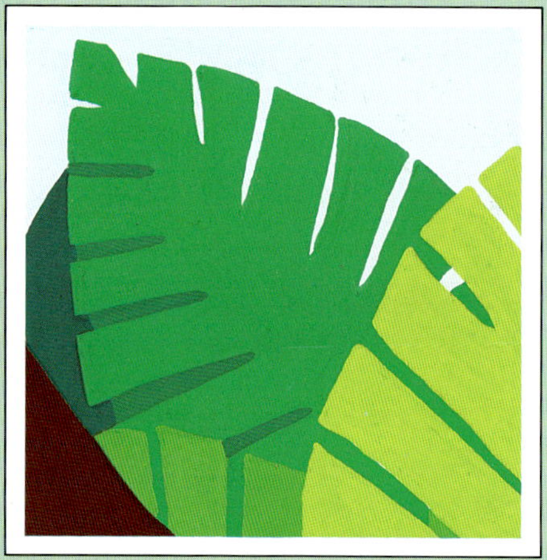